The Sec of Witchfield Academy

Andrew Rafferty

TO Rachael
Hope you enjoy reading
this as much as I enjoyed writing
it
   Andrew

Copyright © 2016 Andrew Rafferty

All rights reserved, including the right to reproduce this book, or portions thereof in any form. No part of this text may be reproduced, transmitted, downloaded, decompiled, reverse engineered, or stored, in any form or introduced into any information storage and retrieval system, in any form or by any means, whether electronic or mechanical without the express written permission of the author.

This is a work of fiction. Names and characters are the product of the author's imagination and any resemblance to actual persons, living or dead, is entirely coincidental.

ISBN: 978-1-326-54864-3

PublishNation
www.publishnation.co.uk

To my mum who never gave up on me and to those who helped me gain the confidence to keep going. You know who you are.

Prologue

They say it is hard being a teenager, having to deal with raging hormones, family dramas and of course the hell that is high school. Pretty much every teenager hates high school. They hate the classes, the teachers, the mountains of homework they are given and sometimes they can't even stand the other students. It is hard dealing with it all, but worse if you're a teenager with uncontrollable powers.

Thankfully there is a place dedicated to the education of young witches and warlocks. Witchfield Academy It is one of the best schools in the world and is classed as a safe haven where the next generation of witches go to learn, focus and ultimately harness their new found powers and abilities. It is like most schools in some respects, like other schools it has students, teachers and classes. Unlike other schools the students are witches and so are the teachers, well some of them anyway, the classes are unique as well to say the least. Instead of doing chemistry you would be mixing potions and instead of English you would be learning and casting spells. The classes may be different and unusual but they are all essential in a young witch's education.

The teachers aren't exactly normal either, some of them are witches, while others are magical creatures, such as gnomes, elves etc. some of the teachers are rather nice, while some are quite scary and the rest are just plain weird. But in the magical world you will get used to it. Well eventually.

This story is about a young girl named Katrina Woods and her amazing journey into the exciting world of magic. At this school she will not only learn spells and potions but she will also learn the dark history of her family and the vital role she will have to play to ensure that history does not repeat itself.

Chapter One

Katrina Woods was your typical high school girl. She was the most popular girl in school, head of the cheerleading squad and the student body president. She had it all: Katrina was your typical teenage beauty with long raven hair, deep emerald eyes that seemed to glow in the light and a cute half cut smile that always seems to light a room, her life was more or less perfect. That is until she turned sixteen. For that is the day everything changed and her life would never be the same again.

Her birthday started out fairly normal; she had breakfast with her parents as usual, the whole time though neither one of them even hinted that they remembered her birthday, which she found strange since it was such a big day for everyone. Trying not to think too much on it, Katrina went to school and afterwards to the mall with her friends. Like her parents, they didn't mention her birthday one little bit.

When Katrina got home the house was in total darkness and her parents had left a note taped to the hallway mirror "*Gone to dinner money for pizza in the dining room*" Katrina looked at the note and was heartbroken, she couldn't believe that no one had remembered her birthday.

Katrina went into the dining room to get the pizza money, the room, like the rest of the house was in total darkness. She felt around for the light switch and finally found it. Once she turned on the light the entire room erupted in bursts of "Surprise" and "Happy Birthday", Katrina let out a banshee like scream and hugged her parents affectionately, smiling and laughing with tears of joy streaming down her face. The party was in full swing when Katrina said to her parents in a tone of pure joy "I can't believe you guys actually managed to surprise me" her mother laughed and said "I know, it's great but we can't take all the credit, your friends helped out too" she gestured to Katrina's friends who were getting rather close to the football team and loving every second of the attention.

The party ran on until near midnight and once everyone had left Katrina's parents sat her down and gave her their gift, completely overrun with excitement Katrina tore off the paper to reveal a long slender box, when she opened it she saw the most astounding necklace she had ever seen. It was a simple white gold chain with a blood red diamond hanging in a stunning iron setting. Katrina just stared at it in sheer bewilderment and finally managed to say

"Oh my god it's amazing I love it thanks you guys". To show her appreciation Katrina gave her parents huge hugs and quickly proceeded to put the necklace on. Her parents smiled and her mother said in a very prideful tone "It belonged to our ancestor Antonia; it gets passed down from mother to daughter when they turn sixteen" Katrina looked at her mother and smiled in awe "And now it's time it was passed down to you" tears filled her eyes as she gave Katrina a warm and loving hug.

Katrina's father finally joined in the conversation "There is one more thing we need to tell you sweetie" Katrina knew it had to be bad, he only ever called her sweetie when it was really bad news "Our family has a secret, a big one" he paused for a moment trying to find the right words, to tell her. He decided just to tell her straight "We are witches and so are you" Katrina looked at her parents and laughed "You're kidding right, please tell me this is some weird joke"; her parents just looked at her and shook their heads, Katrina still wasn't convinced, so to prove it her father went over to the fire place snapped his fingers and said "Fire burn bright I command you ignite", as he finished a green flame appeared in the fireplace. Katrina just sat there in a state of utter shock and managed to say "I'm a witch a real witch I just … I just can't believe it" "I know sweetie" said her mother softly. "No.., no you don't mom, most kids expect a car or cash when they are sixteen, not to be told they are some freak with powers", snapped Katrina in a tone mixed with anger and fear but mostly anger.

Katrina finally calmed down slightly and managed to say to her parents "Why didn't you guys ever tell me" "Oh sweetie we wanted to, but, there is a rule that states that if your child is born in the mortal world then they must be raised mortal until they turn sixteen" explained her mother "Who came up with that rule, it's ridiculous?"

Katrina asked furiously "That would be the council of witches, a bunch of cruel old power mad witches and warlocks, they made up the rule to discourage witches from living on earth, it's stupid but we wanted you to have a normal upbringing even if that meant not having any powers" her mother informed her. Katrina's father knelt down next to her and said in his kindest voice "I know that this is a lot to take in but just know that we will be here if you need us"

"So what now?" asked Katrina trying very hard to hold back her temper. Her mother answered in a nervous voice trying to find the right words, "Well dear, um we knew you would be coming into your powers so we managed to get you a place at Witchfield Academy it's one of the best schools where you can learn to control your new powers and soon you will discover your own unique power"

Katrina was so shocked by this statement she shouted "Wait your telling me I need to switch schools, uh this just gets worse and worse" it was obvious she was upset but she managed to ask one last question before bursting into tears "So when do I have to leave?" "You leave tonight" replied her mother choking up slightly "You will need to pack some things then we will call a portal to send you there". Without saying a word Katrina stormed out and packed a bag and got some personal things to take with her to school.

Katrina returned to the dining room where she saw her parents looking through a very old and weird looking book "Ok what is that thing?" she asked looking confused "This is our family Grimoire, it contains every spell used by our family" replied her mother "Aha found it" called her father pointing to a page in the book. They both joined hands and started chanting "**Mystic forces far and near we call upon you to now appear. Magic portal open wide take her to the other side**". Once they stopped chanting a large blue swirling portal opened up in the archway. Katrina took one last look at her parents and wished them a fond and sad farewell "Bye sweetie" called her mother tears now filling her eyes "Someone will be there to meet you when you get there" called her father, With those final words Katrina stepped through the portal to start an amazing adventure.

Chapter Two

As Katrina emerged from the swirling portal she found herself in a truly grand hall, its walls were covered in portraits depicting what looked to be scenes from fairy tales but they were warped, in the distance was a large window with a breath-taking view of the mountains that seemed to stretch forever, and in the sky a full moon so large that you could almost reach out and touch it. While staring at the amazing sights around her she heard a small but shrill voice calling "Hey girly you're late" she looked around confused hearing a voice but not seeing a body attached to it "Hey missy I'm talking to you" the voice came again, finally, looking down Katrina found the body attached to the voice, a gnome, he looked exactly like the typical garden gnome funny hat and everything, the only difference was the professor robe he was wearing. After a minute of silent staring Katrina finally said "Oh I'm sorry I was distracted, um not to be rude or anything but who are you?"

I am Mr Ignius Muldeywrap the fourth" replied the gnome sounding rather snobbish and proud "But everyone calls me Mr M because they are unable to pronounce my name" he continued this time sounding more angry. Katrina was unsure of what to do now so she simply extended her hand and said "Nice to meet you sir", he did not respond he just glared.

Mr M gestured to Katrina to follow him, obliging she followed him down a long wide hallway that seemed endless "I teach magical literature, you will learn all the books on magic from popular literature" "Oh interesting" replied Katrina not paying any attention to a single word he was saying, mainly because she was so mesmerized by the suits of armour and the vast array of ancient weapons on the wall "*God what is this place a school or an armoury*" she thought now looking slightly worried "Hey girly listen up" Mr M snapped "Now of all the books we will be learning those dreadful *Twilight* books will NOT be among them" he announced raising his voice loud enough to snap Katrina out of her daze.

After what felt like ages they finally reached a large set of wooden doors "Ok girly just go through the door and the headmistress will be waiting for you" Mr M said rather plainly "But there is no handle" replied Katrina pointing to the door rather confused "I said through the door, that means you literally go through the door" replied Mr M now getting very testy. Katrina reluctantly complied, held her breath and walked straight through the doors, on the other side of the doors Katrina found herself in a rather large and extravagant office. She looked over at the desk in the centre of the office and saw a mature delightfully plump woman with bright red hair reading through a veritable mountain of paperwork, with a simple clear of the throat from Katrina the woman looked up from her papers and saw the young girl standing there "Oh you must be the new girl Katrina Woods, I am Ms Amelia Greystone the headmistress of this fine institution it is a pleasure to meet you" she said kindly as she extended her hand knocking some papers over "Nice to meet you too" replied Katrina seeming a little less nervous but not much. Ms Greystone looked at Katrina and saw the slight worry in her eyes "Is something the matter dear you seem out of sorts", "Oh I'm fine" replied Katrina "It's just I'm not exactly sure what I'm doing here" she said in a rather down tone.

Ms Greystone gestured to Katrina to sit then she sat next to her and answered her question the best she could "Simply put dear the main reason you're here is to learn your new powers, you see every witch has the basic powers of potion making and spell casting but each witch has a unique power that eventually manifests itself" "Own unique power?" asked Katrina looking very confused "Yes, for example my power is shape shifting I can become anyone or anything I choose" replied Ms Greystone making her point by quickly turning into a Siamese cat then back to herself. Katrina looked on in shock then managed to snap out of her frozen state to say "Um wow cool trick oh and I think I may have upset that teacher I met when I arrived" "What teacher dear?" asked Ms Greystone confused "Mr M I tried to shake his hand but he just glared at me" replied Katrina sounding worried. Ms Greystone couldn't help chuckle slightly "Oh don't worry dear that's just old Iggy the way he acted towards you is how all gnomes are around witches they don't really trust us not since the lawn gnome incident" "Lawn gnome incident?" Katrina asked now looking extremely confused "A couple of centuries ago an evil old witch caught a gnome and turned him into a statue out of cruelty, then some humans saw it and made copies to sort of mock the gnomes, and to this day they still hold a grudge" said Ms Greystone in mock anger. Katrina sat there in total amazement, she had been a witch for less than a day and found out some amazing things, "Well dear I think you should head to your room and meet your roommate and get some sleep, I will have your schedule sent to you" with that Katrina left the office and went to find her room. After wandering aimlessly through more labyrinths of halls

Katrina finally found her room, a little nervous Katrina went for it and entered the room. Upon her entry she practically knocked her roommate down, "Hey careful there" called the girl from behind the door "Oh I'm so sorry I didn't see you there" replied Katrina who was apologising profusely "Oh its fine, really, I'm Emily your roommate" replied the young girl extending her hand. She was a young girl around Katrina's age, she had a caramel complexion deep hazel eyes and long curled raven hair, she seemed nice; "It's nice to meet you too I'm Katrina, sorry for the door to the face" replied Katrina chuckling slightly. After their introductions Emily gave Katrina a quick tour of the room and showed her where to put her things.

The two girls spent some time gossiping and got to know each other better, all the while Katrina still couldn't get used to the fact that she was a witch, and starting tomorrow she would be learning magic and so much more, "Emily what's it like here?" asked Katrina somewhat nervously. "It's great, a bit weird but great, you'll love it here" replied Emily smiling. The whole time that was being said Katrina was still very nervous. Emily noticed Katrina fiddled with her necklace and noticed the odd glow that emanated from it "Hey nice necklace where did you get it?" she enquired now brimming with curiosity "It was a birthday gift it belonged to one of my ancestors named Antonia" replied Katrina with a strange sense of pride in her words "Wow" replied Emily in amazement "A family talisman those are meant to be really powerful" Katrina was amazed that such a small item had so much power. Later, Katrina finally managed to drift off to sleep unaware that things were about to change forever.

Chapter Three

The sun rose gently in the east and hit Katrina square in the eyes as she slept, she twisted and turned in her bed trying her hardest to avoid the light but she couldn't, it was happening whether she liked it or not. She had to go to class. The two roommates were getting ready for class when a large manila enveloped appeared on Katrina's bed in a rather large puff of smoke, in curiosity the two girls looked at the envelope and saw Katrina's name on it written in a fancy purple scrawl "Ooh fancy wonder who sent it" Emily asked brimming with curiosity "No idea, let's find out" replied Katrina now quite curious herself. She opened the envelope and found inside a note.

Dear Katrina

As promised last night in my office here is your class schedule and a copy of the student manual please ensure you familiarise yourself with it

From

Ms Greystone

Katrina put the note down and grabbed her schedule and found her first class "Well it looks like I have potions first with a Mr Darkholme" she told Emily "Oh tough break honey, he is the nastiest teacher in this place" replied Emily "Good luck girl you'll need it" she called to Katrina as she left for her own class. Katrina just stood for a minute suddenly worried, but she decided to suck it up and go for it.

After going through what seemed to be a veritable maze of stairways and corridors Katrina finally managed to find her classroom , it was as you would suspect for a potion class, located in the dungeon, a bit cliché but it worked. The room was dark, dull and had a most terrible smell of something dead, and it looked like a scene pulled out of a horror film or even a Steven King novel, yet the creep factor made it seem all the more appropriate. Just as Katrina got into the room every other student clamoured to get to their seats, Katrina rushed and found the nearest available seat, as she got to it she nearly threw the guy sitting next to her off his "Oh god I am so sorry I'm so clumsy" exclaimed Katrina "Oh its fine" replied the young man turning to her smiling "No harm done I'm Chris, Chris Summers, it's nice to meet you". Katrina was completely transfixed at the sight of this handsome young man; she thought he was absolutely breath-taking. His hair was like golden sand his eyes a deep shade of ocean blue and a smile that seemed took her breath away, and from what she could see at that angle he defiantly worked out. After staring at him for what felt like forever Katrina finally managed to snap out of daze and reply "I'm Katrina Woods nice to meet you and sorry about the whole nearly knocking you over thing it's a bad habit I'm trying hard to break" Chris smiled "Oh yeah the new girl, I know all about you, you've made quite an impression around here" he said. "Oh really why is that" Katrina asked now very curious "You mean you don't know? Your family are legends, they were part of the biggest war in magical history" replied Chris shocked that Katrina didn't know this about her own family. Katrina just looked at him in shock herself, she was about to ask him what he meant but before she could the teacher entered to start the class.

Mr Darkholme the potion teacher entered the class in such a manner that every single student became deathly silent. Mr Darkholme definitely fit in with the creepiness of his classroom, he was a tall man with long greasy white hair, a very thin face with a long and crooked nose that looked like it had been broken one to many times. He turned to the entire class glaring at each one with his beady eyes saying in a blood curdling voice "Alright class settle down we have a lot to cover today" as he continued scanning the room he noticed Katrina and said in a spine tingling tone "And who are you missy I've never seen you before?"

"Oh. I'm uh, I'm Katrina Woods, I'm new here" Katrina replied stuttering severely which is something she had never done in her life. "Oh yes I know who you are, well you're behind on the work so do try to catch up" retorted Mr Darkholme rather venomously. Mr Darkholme turned his heels and moved to the head of the class and addressed his students "Now class today I shall be demonstrating the enlargement potion" he moved over to a large metal cauldron and took a pipette and removed a small amount of the green bubbling liquid, "Now watch what happens when a few drops are administered to this common lizard" as he said those words he placed three drops of the liquid on the lizard and within a matter of seconds the tiny creature grew and grew till it was a very large size.

The students gazed at the lizard in amazement and began to murmur "All right quiet down, now it's your turn. In front of you are the ingredients you will need to accomplish what I just did" with that the students started working on their potions "But be warned one of the ingredients on the table is wrong and if you add that the results won't be pretty" sneered Mr Darkholme grinning in a rather unseemly way. The students went on working in a way that seemed to indicate that they all knew what they were doing, all that is accept Katrina who just sat there in a state of paralysing fear. Chris saw the state that Katrina was in and gently whispered to her "Don't worry I remember this one I'll help you".

"Thanks I really appreciate it this is just weirdness to me" Katrina replied with a grateful whisper. The two of them set off cutting, peeling and squeezing a vast variety of unusual and disgusting ingredients and tossing them into the small iron cauldrons on their desks. Time was running out and Chris and Katrina were down to the last two ingredients on their desks "Ok so which one do we add?" asked Katrina who had calmed down a little since the start of the class "Um I uh I don't know" replied Chris now nervous "Oh man my mind has gone totally blank" Katrina stared at him and gulped her nerves now returning in spades. Trying to compose herself, Katrina just said calmly "Let's both put one in our cauldrons and see who is right". Nodding in agreement Chris and Katrina both put their respective last ingredients in the cauldrons and whether they liked it or not there was no turning back now.

As the class was drawing to a close Mr Darkholme banged on the cauldron on his desk and called out to the class "Ok times up time to test your potions", with this he walked around the room watching as each student tested their potions, all were so far successful. Then the moment of truth, it was Katrina's turn, Mr Darkholme stood over her glaring down at her with his cold almost lifeless eyes, "Miss Woods it is your turn let's see if you got it right" he said in an almost venomous tone. Katrina took a deep breath and put a single drop of the horrid mixture on her lizard. To her absolute amazement within seconds it grew, and grew and then. BANG. Her lizard exploded right in her face, and the entire class burst out in shrieks of laughter. Once the laughter subsided slightly, the end of class bell rang and Mr Darkholme announced "Alright class dismissed, oh and Miss Woods you have lizard in your hair" the entire class left while Chris and Katrina stayed behind to get cleaned up.

The students clambered out of the class as quick as they could all accept Katrina and Chris who were chatting casually on their way out "Ugh that was the most disgusting thing I've ever seen" announced Katrina shuddering as she said it, "Ha you think that's bad just wait till we have to collect wart puss" replied Chris with a very devious smile on his face. Katrina could tell instantly he was kidding he was cute but a liar he was not, she just smiled back at him in a somewhat flirtatious manner. As they walked down the hall laughing their heads off they ran into Emily who was coming from the opposite direction "Oh hey Emily" called Katrina trying to get her friend's attention "Oh hey" replied Emily somewhat dishevelled "Sorry I was miles off how was your class"? "Well I'm covered in goo from a lizard, so not well" pouted Katrina "Oh you'll get it don't worry" replied Chris, Katrina smiled then remembered Emily was there "Oh sorry Chris, this is Emily my roommate and Emily this is Chris, my potion lab partner"

"Oh it's very nice to meet you Chris" replied Emily now turning on what she thought was charm   "Uh nice to meet you too" replied Chris who was slightly scared of Emily "Oh I gotta run I'll see you at lunch ok" Chris said as he made a quick and classy exit.

Once she was sure that Chris was out of earshot Emily immediately asked "Ok sweetie spill how you bagged Mr Hottie back there"? "I nearly knocked him over with my bag" replied Katrina with a half cut smile, "Ugh now why didn't I think of trying that" replied Emily in mock disappointment. Emily just smiled and said "You know I think he likes you" Now she was blushing, "What no way we just met" replied Katrina trying to throw off Emily's thoughts like they were insane, "Say what you want but I know and he's a great catch" replied Emily rather matter of fact like. Katrina just looked and laughed "I'm serious" replied Emily "It's your first

day and you somehow get the hottest guy in school to basically fall in love with you AND he is a musician AND has the power of nature enchantment " "Uh he has what now" replied Katrina looking at Emily like she suddenly sprouted an extra head "Nature enhancement is a power that allows the person to control and manipulate any form of plant and vegetation, it's a cool trick it's his unique power every witch has one" replied Emily. Katrina decided to get more info on things; she then asked "Ok so what is your special power then?" "My special power is portal creation. I can create portals to anywhere in place or time" Katrina looked at her friend in complete amazement "Wow that's very impressive",
"Yeah it is but I gotta run see you later" Emily called running down the hall. Katrina was totally amazed and overwhelmed by this information, every witch had a unique power and if that was true then what would hers be. And Emily was under the impression that Chris was in love with her. In all this Katrina didn't realise she was late for her next class.

The rest of Katrina's first day went about as good as potions did, which was not so good at all. Right after potions she had basic spell casting, which was taught by Ms Lyre a small portly witch whose face looked like a squashed pigeon. The lesson was levitation, the object of the lesson was to levitate some books to a shelf nearby, when Katrina tried it however she sent her desk flying through a stained glass window. Her flying class was even worse, while the rest of the class soared with a kind of grace she was trying to get out of a tree she somehow found herself in. the flying teacher was not that impressed but he couldn't help laughing a little, that is until the broom did a turn and flew straight through another stained glass window.

Her magical literature class was by far the most embarrassing of all, it was taught by Mr M the ill-tempered gnome she met the day she arrived. Little did she realise the class lived up to its name all the books were enchanted so when they were opened they came to life, Katrina foolishly opened a copy of *The Wizard of Oz* and unleashed a hoard of flying monkeys on the class. Which flew around terrifying everyone then flew through another of the schools stained glass windows.

By the time lunch came around Katrina was totally dishevelled but perked up quite considerably upon seeing Chris, "Hey Katrina over here" he said gesturing to the table, as she walked over she noticed he had changed his clothes now instead of the shirt and jeans he was wearing this morning , he was wearing a grey vest which showed off his chest and arm muscles perfectly, he also wore a pair of jogging trousers that fit him perfectly in all the right places "Hey Chris what's with the change of clothes couldn't get the lizard out huh" she said in a very gloomy tone "No I just came from magic combat class that's why I'm wearing these" he said in a reassuring tone "You ok you seem kind of down". "Oh yeah I just don't think I'm cut out to be a witch" replied Katrina now sounding very depressed "Oh don't be silly you're just new it takes time to learn this stuff believe me" Chris said trying in vain to cheer Katrina up even in the slightest "Yeah right I stink I mean I blow up a lizard, fly my desk out a window, get stuck in a tree and let loose a load of flying monkeys on my class" Chris looked at her and burst out In laughter "It's not funny" said Katrina in a near shout "Sorry but it kind of is I mean flying monkeys that's hilarious", Katrina just looked at Chris in a way that was extremely venomous.

Then without any warning a loud clap of thunder filled the room "What was that?" called Katrina not realising she was clinging onto Chris trembling in fear, "No idea, there hasn't been a cloud in the sky all day" replied Chris. Just as he said it another loud clap of thunder and Katrina gripped Chris even tighter, that is until she finally realised it and quickly released her near death grip, "Sorry I really hate thunder storms they freak me out" said Katrina turning a bright shade of Magenta "Its ok I don't mind" replied Chris with a kind smile. As they exchanged looks Katrina saw the picture behind Chris moving as if being hit by a storm "Wow I don't know the pictures here moved" announced Katrina I'm pure amazement "They don't normally" replied Chris confused, As they stared at the picture in astonishment the storm suddenly seemed to subside. They both exchanged amazed looks then Chris realised something "You're not upset anymore" he said to Katrina "So I'm not upset anymore what's that got to do with anything?" she asked Chris very confused "When you were upset the storm started, and when I helped calm you down the storm subsided" said Chris. Katrina just looked at him like he was talking gibberish "You can project your emotions and bring them out in art work, that's very rare" he continued. Katrina sat there in shock, she knew she would get her own power but she had no idea it would be so powerful. Things were going to get a lot more interesting.

Chapter Four

It was coming up to the end of Katrina's second week at school and she was getting better, she wasn't messing up as much in her classes, except potions which she still was terrible at, of course Mr Darkholme's nasty personality didn't help. But at least Chris was there to help, though he was more like a very welcome distraction. The school was buzzing with preparations for Halloween, a very power and spiritual time for witches, and it was also time for a little fun. As per the tradition of Witchfield Academy the students would get Halloween off to have fun, there would be stalls and booths set up all over the school and after sunset there would be a costume party, which really let the students go wild in all respects.

When Halloween finally came around Katrina wasn't exactly in a cheery mood, seeing her like this her new best friend Emily decided to investigate "All right girl spill, you've been little miss downer for days"

"Oh it's nothing really" replied Katrina sounding very unconvincing, knowing that statement to be false Emily gave her the old *I don't believe you* stare and within seconds Katrina crumbled "Alright fine, I've had some bad experiences with Halloween, a few years ago the guy I was dating dumped me at a costume party" she said solemnly "Wow that really sucks" replied Emily "But that was then this is now, we are going to that party and you will have fun even if I have to force you" Katrina just smiled and gave her friend a thankful hug. The two friends used their time very wisely, they went to find costumes for the party, the school had an unusually high surplus of costumes and the girls took full advantage.

After trying on many different costumes Katrina finally found the perfect one stashed in an old trunk in the back of the room, it was simple yet elegant. A full length blue silk gown that seemed to shimmer in the light, it came with a long see through flowing cloak "Wow you look amazing" Emily said looking very impressed with the outfit "Really I feel kind of weird in this" replied Katrina sounding very self-conscious "Are you nuts you look amazing, you're like a fairy tale queen in that dress" replied Emily trying to reassure her friend. It took some time but Katrina finally caved in "Fine I will wear the dress but you need to wear something too" "Oh don't worry I know exactly who I'm going as" Emily smiled "I just need to go and pick it up"

"Ok I'll see you back at the room" replied Katrina and with that they went off.

It was almost time for the party and Katrina was seriously on the fence about whether or not to go "Oh we've been over this you look amazing" urged Emily "I just feel really weird wearing this" replied Katrina very apprehensively "Come on I told Chris you were going and he is dying to see you in your costume" Katrina was amazed it only took Emily a few weeks to know her weak spot "You are evil you know that right" Katrina said jabbing her friend in the side "Oh you have no idea" Emily said smiling. Once the girls were ready they went down to the party, all eyes were on Katrina as she looked stunning in her dress, and Emily looked great too she decided to go as Marilyn Monroe, she had the blond wig and a white dress that she enchanted to blow up every now and then. The two separated and started to mingle, of course Katrina was having a hard time considering her past, but that was soon going to change.

Katrina pushed through a crowd of students to try and reach the punch bowl, but someone pushed back and she fell herself falling, but within seconds the sensation stopped she didn't fall she was just suspended in mid-air. Getting rather freaked out by the whole floating thing Katrina yelled "Oh god whoever did this please let me go", Chris walked through the crowd, stood behind Katrina and simply said "Release" with that Katrina started her fall again but landed in Chris' arms "Um nice catch" Katrina said blushing at the fact she just said that "My pleasure" Chris replied smiling, after a few seconds Katrina managed to say "Love the costume it looks great on you" Katrina was only saying this because she thought he looked hot in his outfit, Chris decided to dress as a genie. His costume was the classic genie look baggy blue pants, funny turban and a waist coat; to be honest he wasn't wearing a shirt so he was able to show off his muscular arms and his six-pack, which Katrina didn't mind at all. After the coy smiles were over with Chris broke the ice by saying "So care to make a wish" he then gave a genie like bow "Maybe later but for now let's just chill" Katrina replied smiling flirtatiously.

After a lot of shameless flirting Chris finally managed to convince Katrina to dance, still pretty reluctant Katrina bit the bullet and followed him to the dance floor. As they arrived the song changed from a loud rock ballad to a slow romantic sway song, hearing this Katrina tried to flee from the dance floor but Chris stopped her "Oh no you don't, you owe me a dance" he said with a charming smile .Just as they started dancing something odd happened, Katrina suddenly felt dizzy, once it passed Katrina looked around and to her shock she was in her past "Oh no not here" she thought to herself, not now. In pure shock Katrina looked around and saw her ex- boyfriend Jordan coming towards her, try as she might she couldn't move "Ah Katrina I'm glad I found you we need to talk" whispered Jordan, she knew what was coming next and she couldn't stop it. Just as he was about to finish Chris' voice echoed and broke through the dream scenario, Katrina looked at Chris shaking violently at the terrifying sight she just saw "Hey are you ok what just happened there" Katrina could only stare at him still in fear, she couldn't say anything she just ran off tears streaming down her face.

As Katrina ran she found herself down an unknown hall at a dead end, not caring one bit she slid down the wall and starting crying loudly and shaking uncontrollably. It didn't take Chris long to find her, and once he did he just sat next to her and comforted her "So what was that back there in the dance hall you kind of zoned" he asked once he was sure she was calm "I don't know, it was weird I saw my ex-boyfriend and he was giving me the same speech as when we broke up at a Halloween party two years ago" Katrina replied more calmly but still shaken. Chris was in shock "Wow that must have been awful but I don't see how you could have seen that, only a powerful mind warping spell could do that" Katrina was shocked now too "Who would do that to me?" "No idea but they are obviously not good" replied Chris. Katrina just sat there now very nervous. Seeing this Chris gave one of his best caring and compassionate hugs which Katrina accepted, little did they know someone was watching them, the unknown force behind the spell.

Chapter 5

Several weeks had passed and Katrina had finally gotten used to being a witch, she was even doing better in her classes. All accept potions this was still a huge problem for Katrina, but it was only because Mr Darkholme purposely made it hard just to be nasty. Apart from that things were looking up; Katrina was starting to get the hang of her new power, but best of all her and Chris were getting much closer. They spent every spare moment they could together, either studying or just hanging out, when she wasn't with Chris she was with Emily her new best friend, yes things were most certainly looking up.

It was coming up to the Christmas break and Katrina decided to stay at school over the break, after hours of debating with herself and practicing in front of the mirror she finally decided to make the call. It was an easy enough calling spell, Katrina stood over the crystal ball on her desk and began chanting **"Magic forces I ask of thee call the one I wish to see"** and to Katrina's amazement the spell actually worked. A small whirl of smoke formed in the crystal and in seconds her parents appeared "Hi mom hi dad" Katrina called into the crystal "Oh hi sweetie how are you?" called her mother so glad just to hear her daughters voice, "I'm good mom I was just calling to let you guys know I'm going to be staying at school over vacation"

"Wait you want to do what" called back her mother in utter dismay "But it's your first Christmas as a witch and the whole family will be here, even your great aunt Agnes"

"Look I know it's a big deal but I really want to stay I really need to catch up on some stuff, plus I won't be alone my roommate Emily will be here and so will Chris" replied Katrina trying to reassure her parents and convince them to let her stay.

Her father finally entered the conversation being the only one who noticed his daughters slip up about mentioning a boy "And who may I ask is this Chris young lady?" he asked in the classic and cliché over protective tone of a father, Katrina stuttered for a moment then said "He's just a really nice guy from class"

"Oh so is he your boyfriend then?" asked Katrina's mother not even noticing her husband and daughter both went a curious shade of red, " No mom he is not my boyfriend but I wouldn't mind if he was" replied Katrina in a mixed tone of happiness and embarrassment. After debating with her parents for almost a full hour she finally convinced her parents to let her stay, but her father gave the old *if he does anything to hurt you I will hurl a lightning bolt at him* speech. Her parents finally hung up and promised to send her presents through the witch mail. It was the day before Christmas and Katrina, Emily and Chris were among the very few students who stayed behind for the Christmas holidays, and each of them had their own reason to want to stay. Emily didn't want to go home because she wasn't into Christmas. The downside was her parents were into it in a big way. Every year they decorated the house like Santa's grotto and they always wore the same hideous matching sweaters, this year though Emily lied to her parents and told them she had detention over the break, any excuse to not wear that sweater.

The reason Chris didn't want to go home was very different, he liked Christmas, and he just didn't like spending time with his family. Every Christmas without fail the family would fight big time and the proverbial fur would fly, and so would the food. When his family start to lose their temper their magic gets out of control and things fly. So this year Chris "Forgot" to request Christmas at home and since it was too late to do anything he was stuck at school. Just, as he had planned.

Katrina's reason for not wanting to go home was pretty much the same as Chris, she loved the season, that wasn't the problem, no, what she couldn't stand was the yearly visit from her least favourite relative, Great Aunt Agnes. Aunt Agnes was a large round woman, oh she was as sweet anything but she had two major flaws. The first was her unnaturally loud voice, Aunt Agnes used to be a famous opera singer, and though she was retired her voice was still pristine. Whenever she laughed or on rare occasions screamed, her voice would get so high that any items made of glass or indeed any breakable substance would shake and in some cases shatter into tiny pieces. Her other flaw was that she was a notorious cheek pincher, every time she visited Katrina's cheeks would be red raw from all the incessant pinching. So Katrina simply said she wanted to spend the holidays with her friends, which was the truth, but a Christmas without Aunt Agnes pinching her cheeks. Big bonus.

The three friends decided to spend some down time in the common room; Chris and Katrina used that opportunity to snuggle up by the fire, the whole time Emily just sat there watching the sickening love scene. Noticing that Emily was getting left out Katrina blurted out the first thing that popped into her head "So what was everyone's worst Christmas memory?" totally confused by the random statement Chris and Emily just looked and Katrina like she had totally lost her marbles, but thought it would be fun and decided to play along.

Emily decided to go first and get her tale of shame and embarrassment over and done with "As both of you know my parents are into Christmas in a big way" the two nodded but had an idea of where this was going "Well a few years ago my parents dressed up as Santa and Mrs Clause for the towns Christmas fair and.." she trailed off "They made me dress up as an elf to amuse the kids, ears and all", there was a dead silence then Katrina and Chris burst out in fits of laughter "Come on it's not funny" called Emily laughing slightly herself "Your kidding right it's hilarious" replied Chris. After the laughter died down Chris decide to go next "Well last year my family got together for our usual Christmas dinner and near the end of the meal my mum said something that annoyed my uncle", the girls looked wondering what was coming next "Well the argument got so heated that my uncles temper got so bad that he caused the Christmas pudding to explode, to this day there is still a big stain on the ceiling" the girls just looked at him and started laughing to which Chris quickly joined in. Finally it was Katrina's turn to give her story "About two years ago we had the whole family over for Christmas" began Katrina "including my little cousin Elliot who is a terror to say the least, well just after dinner we all exchanged gifts and he gave one to Aunt Agnes" Chris and Emily knew where this was headed but let her continue "So Aunt Agnes opens her gift to find a lovely jewellery box, naturally we all think the little brat turned over a new leaf, boy were we wrong, she opens the box and inside was a dead rat. Then she let out a huge scream, one that was so loud that she shattered every window in the room" Emily and Chris looked in mock shock "Wow" said Emily "Its official you win" said Chris giving her a winning smile. The three spent the rest of the day laughing and having a good time, their fun ran late into the night until they finally gave up and went to bed.

The sun rose gently in the sky the next day rousing Katrina from her deep sleep, after being properly woken Katrina realised why she was up so early, it was Christmas Morning. In excitement Katrina and Emily ran down to the common room still in their pyjamas, Chris was already there waiting for them still looking half asleep. The three friends spent the first couple of hours enjoying the assortment of Christmas treats and having fun with the magical exploding Christmas crackers, and the novelty gifts that came with them. Once the food was out of the way, untouched mostly accept for the pies which Chris took care of they decided to get to the best part of the day. Presents. The gifts were of course kept under the tree, cliché yes but it was a quaint tradition, they went over grabbed their respective gifts and made their way to the comfortable sofas which were almost always filled by other students. Once they got to their seats they got into comfortable positions and proceeded to open their gifts.

Emily decided to go first and open her present. She took her first gift a medium sized soft package that was most obviously an item of clothing, Katrina tore the paper off rather excitedly then the excitement quickly faded when she saw what it was "Oh no I don't believe it I can't believe they sent me this" "What is it?" Katrina asked seeing her roommate's horror "Just look" Emily then held up the most hideous looking Christmas sweater anyone could imagine. There was a few moments of silence which was quickly broken by Chris giving a loud snort then bursting into fits of laughter, which Katrina and even Emily quickly joined in "Oh man your parents must be twisted in the head to send you that" Chris said not realising how nasty his statement sounded "I'm sure they meant well, now what else did you get?" Katrina asked trying to minimise the chances of a fight "Just my grandmothers fudge it's not bad but it can make people act weird" replied Emily sounding a bit upset, "So whose going next" she said promptly just to get the attention off of herself.

Chris decided to go next, he decided best open the card from his mother and get the sappy bit over with. With a deep breath Chris opened the card and a small projection of his mother appeared and delivered a rather sweet message "Hi sweetie we are all so sorry you can't make it home for the holidays, but I've sent you some of my fruit cake, enjoy, and your father and I both love you" once the image vanished Chris looked rather pale "What's the matter the message was sweet" Katrina asked confused by the sudden change of face "The message was fine" replied Chris solemnly "It's just, she sent her fruitcake and it is terrible, my mum is a great cook but the family fruitcake always tastes horrible, I just don't have the heart to tell her I don't like it, she would be crushed" Katrina was amazed at what she just heard, it was obvious Chris had a good heart. Chris moved onto his next gift which was from Katrina, he tore the paper off rather excitedly and saw a rather expensive shirt "It's to replace the one I ruined during our first potions class" Chris just smiled for a moment then said "Oh this is so nice I love it thanks" he then proceeded to give Katrina a very thankful hug, to which she promptly blushed at.

Finally it was Katrina's turn to open her gifts. She was very excited to see what she got and decided to go for the big one her parents sent, feeling like a kid again Katrina tore off he paper to find to her true surprise a very old a weird looking book "Ok this is a weird gift" Katrina said then noticed the looks her friends were giving her, confused by the looks she was receiving she decided to read the card from her mother hoping to get some clue as to her gift. After rummaging through the paper Katrina found the card which read "*Just though you should have one of your own love Mum and Dad xx*" it took a moment but then Katrina realised what it was, she opened up the book and saw pages littered with spells, potions and all manner of amazing things. It was her very own Grimoire. After seeing the amazing gift she received Chris said "Wow your own Grimoire makes my gift seem kind of lame"

"Wait you got me a gift" Katrina said starting to go pink in the face "Um well yeah, here you go" Chris said handing her the gift now going a bit red himself. Katrina took his gift and carefully opened it, wondering what it could be. When she finally opened it she saw to her amazement and delight a beautiful hand crafted box with intricate designs around it "Oh my gosh it's beautiful I absolutely love it, where did you get it?" asked Katrina overwhelmed with joy "I didn't buy it I made it for you" Chris replied smiling his usual charming smile. Katrina looked at her gift in amazement and just couldn't find the words to say how grateful she was "It gets better, open it and think of your favourite song" Chris instructed, Katrina did as instructed and opened the box and to her amazement her favourite song *Defying Gravity* was playing from the box "That's amazing but how?" Katrina asked amazed by this "It's a charm I placed on the box it plays whatever song your thinking of" Chris explained, Katrina didn't need to hear any more she knew this was the best gift she had ever gotten.

Chapter 6

The day drew on and most of the food still lay untouched except for the mince pies which Chris managed to wolf down in a near instant. Katrina gazed into the fire and basked in its warm comforting glow, as her mind swirled with random thoughts one seemed to push its way into the front of her mind, once it had fully formed Katrina turned to Chris and said "When we met you mentioned that my family were part of some big war what did you mean"

"Oh yeah I totally forgot about that" replied Chris "yeah one of your family members saved the whole magic realm I think there is a book on it in here somewhere" "Don't trust those things they are vague and never give the full story" Emily retorted sounding rather venomous. Chris looked at her rather harshly and said "it's fine I can tell the story, I remembered it from magical history" this said rather proudly, and with that he began the tale of the great magic war

It was around five hundred years previous the realm of magic was a truly beautiful place, that is until she arrived. The dark witch, the nastiest and most vile witch who ever walked the earth. With her army of dark creatures and vicious demons, they ravaged the land and destroyed anything and anyone who got in their way. The people tried to fight her off but those who faced her either wound up dead or as one of her dark thralls, that's how powerful she was. All seemed lost until one powerful witch named Antonia confronted the entire army, as they advanced she used her light magic and banished the entire dark army back to the shadowy depths, only one foe remained, the dark witch. These two mighty women became locked in a battle for power but Antonia was ultimately the victor, with one final spell she obliterated the dark witch and was able to restore all that she had destroyed. There was however a cost, a spell that powerful used up all of Antonia's powers and she ultimately died in order to save everyone.

Katrina and Emily sat there in silence and awe Chris noticed Katrina was in a state of shock and gave her a hug to comfort her "Thanks I needed that, it's bizarre to think that my ancestor single-handedly saved the whole magical realm" Katrina said taking in Chris' warm embrace "I know right she was pretty awesome I guess it runs in the family" Chris said this time without a single sign of embarrassment. Emily who was a bit left out at this point decided to enter the conversation "So how did Antonia's daughter get the necklace, I always thought those things had to be passed down directly?"

"Well that is true" replied Chris "But in cases like that a benefactor is chosen to hold onto the necklace until the heir is old enough to receive the power"

"Oh kind of like a trust fund" Katrina replied getting the gist of what was being said ,"Yeah kind of like that" replied Chris shooting a devilish half cut smile.

As the day grew further on Emily was getting very bored and decided to have a little bit of fun with Katrina and Chris, thinking for a moment on what she could do she decided to use the nearest thing to hand "Hey Chris care for a piece of my granny's fudge" she said sounding oh so innocent "Yeah sure I love fudge" Chris replied unaware of what he was walking into. Chris took a big piece of the fudge and quickly wolfed it down, once he did he began to feel dizzy like he was going to pass out, thankfully though he didn't but the end result was much worse. After regaining his composure Chris calmly walked over to Emily grabbed her waist then dipped her and gave her a kiss that was straight out of an old movie. On seeing the horrible sight in front of her Katrina screamed at both of them "I can't believe this how could you I thought we were friends". On seeing this reaction Emily simply said "Oh well better luck next time" and smiled as Katrina ran out the door crying, and, her cries of sadness managed to break Chris out of the sweets spell and Emily's tight embrace.

Katrina ran down the corridor crying her eyes out and upon hearing Chris coming towards her she pulled up her nerve and slapped him the second he came into range. "Ow what was that for?" enquired Chris now rubbing his sore jaw "Oh you know what that was for you jerk" replied Katrina now brimming with rage "You play these games flirting with me giving me nice gifts and then you go and kiss Emily" Chris laughed for a second and said "Your kidding right I'm not interested in Emily the only reason I did that was because of some fudge she gave me" "Wait you mean the fudge that makes people act weird?" Katrina asked now getting angry again, Chris just nodded in confirmation. Seeing the rage burn in Katrina's eyes Chris thought it best to finally say what he wanted to "Like I said I'm not interested in Emily you're the one I really like" "really?" Katrina asked not knowing whether or not to believe him, "yes really I've had a thing for you since the day we met you're the only girl I think about" Chris replied now fuelled by truth and passion. Katrina still didn't look convinced so Chris did the only thing he could think of, in an instant he pulled Katrina in by the waist and gave her a kiss so true and passionate that all the lights in the immediate vicinity exploded into bursts of colourful fireworks and as the two of them were surrounded by this beauty their passion caused them to float a few inches of the ground. After what felt like a blissful eternity the kiss broke and Katrina managed to say while still catching her breath "Wow you certainly know how to get your point across" Chris just smiled and said "now that my point is across Katrina will you be my girlfriend"

"What do you think" Katrina said as she gave Chris another passion filled kiss this time minus the fireworks.

Chapter 7

The new semester had started and Chris and Katrina were now officially a couple, which was great but Katrina and Emily still hadn't said a word to each other after the Christmas incident. It was Katrina's first class of the new semester, Divination the dullest class in the entire school, at least that's what the students thought, the teachers on the other hand found it ridiculous and outdated but Ms Greystone kept it around for tradition.

The teacher Ms Oswald was not like the rest of the staff not by a long shot, she had wild untamed hair which constantly housed her *misplaced* glasses. She always seemed to talk in riddles or just absolute nonsense. Over the years rumours had circulated the school that she was once a great seer until an evil witch dug out her mind because she saw something she shouldn't have, but it was just never proven.

As the students entered they all looked half asleep except Katrina who was all giddy with love. The class had begun and Ms Oswald rose from an incredibly overstuffed chair at the head of the class and announced in a very dazed voice "Welcome future oracles to this divination class, now I don't expect all of you to contain the great force that the sight requires but we shall at least try" the class just looked at each other not sure how to take the obvious mass insult "Now we shall be focusing on using the crystal ball for now and later we shall use the runes" she continued gesturing to the tables "Let us start off by you all focusing on the crystals for a bit to see if you can get connected" with that the students went to try and use the crystal balls as instructed.

The students went to work, though most of them weren't even trying because they didn't see the point of the class, but somehow it was working for Katrina. She wasn't even trying but somehow the crystal ball she was staring into started glowing and at its heart she could see Chris "Wow I did it I can't believe it" even though she said this under her breath somehow Ms Oswald heard her and within seconds she was right next to her "Oh my, well done my dear it seems your feelings towards this young man has pulled back the veil of the universe and allowed you to make contact" Katrina was nodding but not really listening as she was transfixed on Chris. She still couldn't believe it she just stared into the crystal more mystified by the second, there was Chris in his chants class and it looked like he was singing but Katrina couldn't here. Then within seconds the crystal changed again this time a sinister black smoke filled the orb and a voice echoed from it "Be warned child she is almost here the dark one is almost here she will come for you she will COME" the voice then became a shrill tone which so intense that the crystal ball shook and shattered into thousands of tiny pieces. The entire class heard the shattering and all quickly turned in Katrina's direction, seeing this Ms Oswald quickly rose from her chair and announced "All right everyone that is enough for today it seems the mystic veil has closed now everyone grab your things and go", everyone silently got there things and left all except Katrina who just sat there shaking "My dear are you alright you seem shaken up" Ms Oswald asked noticing Katrina's worry "Oh yeah I'm fine" Katrina replied "My dear you have many talents but lying isn't one of them now stay back for a bit and have some chamomile tea to relax you" Katrina did as instructed and stayed back while there she did relax a little and explained it all to Ms Oswald who believed it was a spiritual omen and by the results not a good one. Hearing that Katrina finished her tea made her excuses and left as fast as she could.

It was lunch time and Katrina was pacing the main entrance her nerves getting worse with each lap when Chris turned up and spoke "Hey are you ok you seem kind of wired"

"oh yeah I'm fine" retorted Katrina sarcastically "Unless you count the fact that earlier some crazy ghost made contact with me and warned me that someone was after me, I mean I've only been a witch for a few months I couldn't have made anyone this mad already could I?" after her little speech Katrina started hyperventilating, seeing how upset she was getting took her deep in his arms and gave her a wonderfully soothing hug and said gently in her ear "Don't worry I'm sure it was nothing just a crossed wire" "Yeah right" snorted Katrina in severe disbelief "One minute I'm watching you in your charm class then this weird voice takes over and says I'm in danger hardly a crossed wire"

"Wait a minute you were watching me while I was in class I'm flattered" Chris replied with a cheeky smile on his face "That is not the point" replied Katrina who was turning an awkward shade of pink "the point is some crazy spirit sent me a warning and I'm not going to ignore it" with that Katrina stormed off her eyes burning with determination.

It had been several days and Katrina was a wreck, she hadn't gotten any sleep after the incident in divination anytime she closed her eyes all she could see was the black smoke and hear the shrill voice repeating the warning over and over. It was a Saturday and Katrina decided to go for a walk in an attempt to clear her head, as she walked around the school grounds she heard a man singing a wonderful song that she had never heard before. Now overcome with curiosity Katrina followed the voice and found at its source, Chris, and as he sang all the plants and flowers around him seemed to burst to life. Once he was finished Katrina finally spoke "You play beautifully I've never heard anything like that" "well I sure hope not" replied Chris laughing "I wrote it I didn't think anyone was listening I like being out here it helps me think plus it helps my power work" "yes I noticed" Katrina replied pointing to the flowers. The two of them sat for a little talking about different things then Chris plucked a tiny flower from a nearby bush and gave it to Katrina, it was sweet but Katrina wondered why he gave her something so tiny. Seeing the confusion Chris hummed a sweet little tune and to Katrina's amazement the flower grew and bloomed in her hand "Wow neat trick" she said smiling "It's sweet I love it" "Well if you like that you'll love this" Chris said and within seconds he was singing again this time a very different song, it seemed to send out vibrations of joy and happiness. As Chris sang all the plant life around him seemed to come to life as if the music was commanding it, seeing this Katrina was astounded that anyone could do something this wonderful. When the song was finished Katrina and Chris were standing in a veritable garden of Eden "Wow that was amazing so who inspired that song?" Katrina asked amazed at what was around her "You did" Chris admitted smiling "After we met I was hit with inspiration and I just started writing and before I knew it I'd written this amazing song, you Katrina are my muse you inspire me like no one else" Katrina just smiled at him not sure how to respond, the two sat and basked in the happiness that they brought each other blissfully unaware that a more sinister force was watching.

The sinister figure in question stood in a very dimly lit room gazing into a cauldron of bubbling green ooze and in a surprisingly young voice said "Oh you simple fools enjoy the moment while you can for soon it will be over" then a loud crack of thunder and flash of lightning struck the cauldron sending it to its two unsuspecting victims. The lightning struck with a loud bang only a few feet from Katrina and Chris who were both now in a state of shock. Chris grabbed Katrina and held her close allowing his steady heartbeat to offer some comfort, once he was sure she was ok he asked "are you ok that was kind of close" "yeah I think so" replied Katrina still shaking slightly, it was obvious she wasn't but after what just happened Chris didn't argue he just held her closer and tried his best to be a comfort. After all she was going to need all the comfort she could get.

Chapter 8

The next day Chris who was still shaken up after the near miss with the lightning decided to find Katrina and make sure she was ok. He asked a few other students and one finally pointed him in the direction of the library, it took Chris a while to get to the library as it was a place he rarely spent any time. It was easy to find Katrina in there as she was sitting in centre of the room surrounded by a large pile of spell books "Bit of light reading?" Chris asked sneaking up behind Katrina and scaring her out of her daze "Oh hey I was just doing some research" she replied looking rather frazzled "Research on what?" enquired Chris sounding both curious and concerned "On whoever or whatever attacked us I'm looking for a spell to identify them" Katrina replied rather plainly. Chris looked at her very worried "Are you sure that's a good idea those spells can be pretty powerful and they can sometimes be dangerous" "I know and I don't care I'm going to find out who has it in for me now you can either help or go your choice" Katrina replied in a rather nasty tone. Chris decided to help if only to make sure Katrina didn't do anything stupid, after looking through several more books finally found what she was looking for in her own Grimoire "Here I found something *To Identify your Foe* it looks easy enough"

"There is no point trying to talk you out of this is there?" Chris asked already knowing the answer "Nope none" Katrina replied studying the spell.

It took a little time but Katrina managed to get all she needed, she was ready to cast the spell. Katrina placed five blue candles in a circle and in the centre placed a clear crystal, once the candles were lit Katrina took a moment to compose herself and began chanting "**Spirit gracious hear my rhyme send this spell back through time. Darkness looms upon this place show my enemy's true face. Spirit mighty I call to thee reveal the dark identity**" the spell was done and within seconds a magical wind whipped the air and from the smoke filled crystal the evils true face was revealed. It was Emily.

Once the shock of their discovery wore off Chris and Katrina ran frantically through the maze of corridors and found themselves at Ms Greystones office. Completely ignoring any manners they possessed the two students walked straight into office unannounced, once inside they both noticed almost immediately the entire staff were looking at them and not all with nice looks either "Miss Woods Mr Summers what is the meaning of this intrusion" Ms Greystone bellowed her voice going a full octave above its usual tone. The two stood in silence for a moment until Chris decided to break the silence and explain "We were attacked yesterday" there were sudden gasps and murmurs from the staff "A bolt of green lighting barely missed us and Katrina just cast a spell to find out who did it and…" he trailed off seeing the looks he was getting "Yes Mr Summers go on we are all dying to hear this" retorted Mr Darkholme sounding more sarcastic than normal "The spell showed that the one who cast the spell was Katrina's roommate Emily" he finished. On hearing this Ms Greystone dismissed the meeting and all the teachers teleported out of the room ,"Now are you sure about it being Emily dear as this is a very serious accusation" Ms Greystone asked "Yes I'm sure the spell defiantly showed Emily there couldn't have been any error" Katrina replied sounding very sure. "Well then we will need to call the council to send someone to take Emily away she is too big a risk" Ms Greystone replied now sounding very serious. Before anything could be done the mirror on the back wall of the office began glowing and in it appeared Emily "Don't bother calling in those old wind bags I'm out of here" she called "Oh and Katrina be seeing you soon" with that she gave a shrill and evil laugh and vanished from the mirror shattering it in the process. Now Katrina was really scared her best friend had just become her worst enemy.

It had been over a week and there was still no sign of Emily so for once Katrina had her guard down. Though she would soon wish she hadn't. It was a particularly dull and rainy Monday morning and Ms Lyre the spells teacher was droning on giving a particularly dull lesson on basic household spells. Katrina like the rest of the class just tuned her out not that she even noticed, she just liked the sound of her own voice, diving deeper into her own head Katrina had started to daydream. Her daydream was very vivid and extremely specific, her and Chris, specifically their romantic moments. The images were of every subtle flirt, every coy smile and in full video format their first passion filled kiss at Christmas, it even included their latest romantic moment in the gardens minus the lightning bolt. Seconds later Katrina was snapped out of her love infested dream and was hurled back into reality. The reason this happened was because the entire class was laughing hysterically which was very odd for this class, Katrina wondered why they were laughing then to her horror she saw it, her dream it was floating in the air in full colour and worst of all it was on a loop. Katrina was utterly mortified, her most personal and intimate thoughts on view for everyone to see, mortified by this Katrina just threw her hands up and to everyone's amazement she vanished in a puff of white smoke

Katrina finally materialized from the smoke and gave a sigh of relief that she was away from all the laughter, her relief was short lived once she realised she was right in the middle of the headmistresses office "Miss Woods what on earth are you doing here" Ms Greystone asked looking rather perplexed "Oh I'm sorry I just had to get away from class" Katrina answered getting rather upset "Oh my dear what on earth is the matter" Ms Greystone asked seeing Katrina getting so upset "Well I was in class and I was daydreaming and…" Katrina trailed off getting more upset again "And your dreams manifested and could be seen by everyone that was Ms Lyres doing she created that spell years ago it's to make sure students pay attention I've been telling her to get rid of it but she refuses" Ms Greystone admitted. After hearing this Katrina was no longer upset but angry "That is terrible so my most intimate thoughts were on display as some kind of punishment it's horrible I'm a laughing stalk" "Yes I understand you are upset but I don't think they will be talking about it much" Ms Greystone said very assuredly, but Katrina didn't get it "When you left the class you teleported in smoke that is advanced magic someone of your age and power level shouldn't be able to do that" Katrina looked her in pure amazement she didn't even notice she did it "Now tell me dear who is your tutor?" Ms Greystone asked and again Katrina had no clue what she was talking about "For your power it has come in right" "Um yes I can make artwork come to life" Katrina replied in a way that made it seem like nothing. Ms Greystone looked in amazement "Well I am shocked your training hasn't begun a great error on the schools part which I will remedy by training you myself and I am very impressed that someone so young has such a unique ability only a few people ever displayed that power" she said brimming with excitement "Now we will begin in a few days I will send you word" and with that Katrina's training was about to begin and it seemed her trainer was more excited than her.

A few days after the daydreaming incident in spells class Katrina finally started her formal training with Ms Greystone, the training took place in a special annex of the school that adapted to the needs of the trainer. As they reached the centre of the room Katrina just said "Wow big place" her voice echoing with each word "Impressive right it's a magic room that can become whatever is needed for the training" Katrina just smiled but deep down was far from impressed. Seeing the lack of her students enthusiasm Ms Greystone decided to step things up a bit "**Oh mystic room vast and strange I command you now to change**" with the uttering of the spell the entire room warped and contorted until it settled down to what looked like a gallery. The room looked very much like a gallery from a museum but was very different instead of statues the room was filled with odd artefacts and the paintings on the wall depicted scenes from very disturbing parts of history, and they moved. Katrina's head darted from thing to thing trying to take in all the strange and amazing sights around her "What is this place?" she asked now impressed "We call it the gallery it houses our most powerful and precious treasures, of course this is just a projection I wanted to bring you here to show you something that was significant not only to magical history but your personal history" still in awe Katrina followed Ms Greystone.

The two moved through several halls until they came to a full length portrait "So who is this" enquired Katrina still in awe of all that was around her "Take a closer look and find out" Ms Greystone said smiling, Katrina took a closer look at the portrait and was shocked to see the figure in the painting was her exact double "Who what the heck is this" she said trying hard not to freak out "That is your ancestor Antonia, I could see the resemblance the second you walked into my office, your looks the necklace and now your powers it is no coincidence" Ms Greystone replied trying to break all the news at once. Katrina sat at a nearby bench in shock "This is some kind of a joke right?" Ms Greystone didn't reply she just shook her head. The session ended with Katrina's head swimming with new information, and no way of processing. Despite all that the training continued over the next few weeks, it mostly consisted of breathing and relaxing exercises which Katrina couldn't get as anytime she relaxed Emily popped into her head. She desperately needed to relax and rest.

Chapter 9

Valentine's Day was fast approaching and it seemed the entire school had been bitten by the love bug. Everywhere you looked you could see students holding hands, and sharing quick kisses in between class and sharing love filled gazes. Even the teachers were getting into the valentines spirit, Ms Lyre the spells teacher was giving a surprisingly interesting lesson on love spells and the hideous side effects they can have. Ms Oswald the loopy divination teacher was telling the class how to divine for their soulmate with the runes, sadly it didn't work but it was still fun to try. Even Mr Darkholme the lemon faced potion teacher was in the valentine spirit; he was teaching his class how to make a temporary infatuation potion, it did wear off after a couple of hours but it was still an interesting recipe. Yes it seemed everyone was filled with the spirit of love. Everyone that is except Katrina, despise the lack of activity on the Emily front she was still on full alert and wasn't paying much attention to anything else including Chris.

Valentine's Day had finally arrived, this year it was on a Saturday so the students didn't have to worry about class and they could just relax and enjoy the day. Katrina woke early as she did every morning out of habit, but this morning instead of being bombarded by the harsh sunlight there were thousands of tiny white lights swirling around the room. Katrina was amazed by the sight in front of her but was even more surprised when the lights gathered together and became a bouquet of long stem red roses, attached to them was a note which read "For the girl of my dreams a token so small please meet me in the great hall C xx" after reading this Katrina jumped out of bed did a quick change spell and made her way to the great hall. For the first time in her entire time at the school Katrina managed to find her way to the great hall with no issues, taking a moment to compose herself and make sure her hair was ok Katrina walked through the doors and saw Chris standing at the far end of the room wearing a pair of well fit black chinos and a red silk shirt that complemented him very well. Chris also noticed Katrina wearing a full length red sequenced dress that made her seem to shimmer in the light, the two saw each other and didn't have to say anything they just gave each other loving hugs and a wonderfully passionate kiss, after finally leaving each other's embrace they left hand in hand for a wonderful date.

Chris led Katrina from the great hall to the main doors of the school and to her amazement there was a carriage and four white Pegasus horses "Oh wow this is amazing how did you do this" Katrina asked in amazement "I have my ways" Chris said smiling "Just wait this is only the beginning" Chris kept smiling as he helped Katrina into the carriage and gave the driver a nod. Seeing the signal the driver urged the horses and they quickly rose into the air and took off, gliding over the countryside Katrina was overwhelmed by all that was going on. After about an hour the driver finally landed the carriage in front of a large wall of hedges, confused by what was going on Katrina couldn't help ask "Um why are we at a big pile of hedges?"

"Your next surprise is inside" Chris said smiling. Katrina had no idea what he meant there was no way in, Chris walked to the hedge, placed a hand on it and simply said "Gate appear" then to Katrina's surprise the hedge parted to reveal a large wooden gate "Ok I'm kind of impressed" Katrina said smiling   "Just wait there is more" Chris said as he pushed open the gate and guided Katrina in. To Katrina's amazement on the other side of the gate was a truly remarkable garden, there was a narrow winding path with lanterns stretching from one end to the other, and on the grass flurries of multi coloured flowers some she recognised while others looked like they were pulled from Fairy Tales.

Katrina took a moment to process the amazing sights around her "Wow" she said "This is amazing, how did you find this place?"   "I didn't I created it for you" Chris replied while staring longingly into Katrina's eyes "Wait you did all this for me?" Katrina asked a tear in her eye at the amazing gesture he had done for her. "Of course, when I'm with you I feel inspired and I saw this in my mind so I came out here and created it" Chris happily admitted. He took Katrina by the hand and led her to the centre of the garden where a white gazeebo stood with a perfect meal for two. After the meal Chris took Katrina on a romantic walk flowers blooming as they passed, "This was by far the best date ever" Katrina said practically glowing "I'm glad you enjoyed it I wanted this to be perfect because there is something I want to tell you" replied Chris now sounding a little nervous "Ok so what do you want to say" asked Katrina now a bit excited.

Chris turned to Katrina took her by her hands and said with all his heart "Katrina you are the most amazing person I have ever met and from the moment I laid eyes on you I knew you were the one for me. I love you Katrina with all my heart and I always will" Katrina was totally taken back by this but managed to say "I... I love you too" and with that the two shared their most passionate kiss truly sealing their love.

Chapter 10

It was the start of spring and as usual the school was abuzz, the spring equinox had always been a big deal to those in the magical realms. For earth based creatures such as gnomes and wood spirits the equinox was a time for renewal and growth, it was the same for witches it was a time of new hope and celebrating nature, but it was also an excuse to loosen up. In the week coming up to the celebration classes were cancelled as part of the schools tradition, this gave the students the chance to relax, reconnect with their roots and to have fun, namely party. Several groups of students had planned parties all spread out across the week and amazingly none overlapping, and Katrina managed to get invited to every single one. Katrina was amazed by her sudden burst in popularity, in fact in recent weeks her and Chris had become the campus "it" couple, the couple that everyone loved and wanted to be friends with. Katrina found it all a bit odd, but she had to admit she liked it.

    Finally getting a break from her new adoring public Katrina used the opportunity of her time off to explore some of the school, during her exploration she came across an unusually placed door right in the middle of the hall "Weird place for a door wonder where it goes" she said to herself looking at the oddly engraved door. Her curiosity had gotten the better of her and Katrina decided to go into the mystery room, unfortunately the door was jammed so Katrina focused her mind and sent a small energy bolt from her hand and forced the door open "Well that worked" Katrina laughed to herself as she proceeded in, as she went in she saw to her amazement an elegant room with full length mirrors covering each wall "Wow someone sure likes themselves" Katrina joked trying to ease her nerves but sadly it wasn't working she felt very uneased. Feeling very creeped out Katrina decided to make a go for the exit, until she saw something odd in the mirror at the far end of the room. Completely ignoring her instincts to run Katrina went closer and saw to her shock that in the mirror was Emily, Katrina was in shock and didn't say a word and she finally gave into her instincts and ran, but as she did the mirrors she passed shattered. Katrina kept going but wasn't very fast and the shattered mirrors were coming from both sides, then in a moment of pure fear and instinct Katrina threw her hands up and vanished to safety. Katrina emerged from her smoke to find herself not in her room where she intended to be but in Chris' room; it was not exactly what she expected instead of a typical messy teenage boy's room it was surprisingly tidy. The walls were covered in music posters and the his desk was littered with music sheets, Katrina knew what she was about to do was wrong but she decided to look through his music sheets, from what she knew of music which was little the songs were pretty good "See something you like" Chris said from behind Katrina making her jump "Oh I didn't hear you there I'm sorry I was snooping I couldn't resist" Katrina said now very embarrassed and ashamed. Chris looked at her and seeing her sincerity he just smiled and said "Its ok I understand you didn't know where you were so you had to find out but what are you doing here?" "Oh that" Katrina said now rather antsy "Emily turned up again she tried to freak me out and I vanished to get away I misfired on the location again", Chris saw Katrina's worry and gave her one of his best comforting hugs and at that moment Katrina knew she didn't need to worry and just sank deep into the hug feeling better by the second.

That night the students gathered in the common room for the party, the faculty were fully aware of the party but kept a close eye on it just in case. The students were just standing around chatting and making small talk, of course that all changed when Chris and Katrina entered the room. Chris wore tight black jeans and a stylish red and black striped shirt, while Katrina wore a stunning red top cut off at the midriff and a matching full length red skirt with a large slit at one side, both of them looked absolutely amazing and all eyes were on them. Within moments the music started and most of the partygoers started dancing whereas others just stood around talking, Katrina left Chris talking with some of his friends and went to get herself a drink. Upon reaching the refreshment table Katrina decided to be daring and try a magical drink, she thought enchanted punch would be safe enough it was charmed to be any drink you thought of. It sounded good but Katrina wasn't convinced so she tested it by taking two sips thinking of different drinks each time and to her amazement it had changed "Good stuff huh it's a crowd favourite" a random student at the table said "Oh yeah its great I really like it" Katrina replied but before she could take another drink a very uncoordinated student bumped into her and sent her drink flying. Seeing this, the girl she was talking too handed her another drink "Here take this one" "Oh thanks let's hope this one survives" Katrina replied "Oh I certainly hope so, well I better go, bye" the girl replied before going, Katrina thought she was nice if not a bit weird. Making sure no one was around Katrina managed to take a large gulp of her new drink, little did she know that the drink had been dosed with a very nasty potion whose effects were about to become very apparent.

It only took a few moments for the potion to take kick in, and the effects were far from good. Katrina was going around the party stumbling over everything and slurring her words whenever she tried to talk, seeing this Chris decided to intervene "Katrina are you ok you seem kind of wasted" Katrina just looked at him and managed to say "Um I don't feel so good". Just after that the real effect of the potion took hold. A strong and painful surge of energy surged through Katrina's body and before she could recover her vision became very distorted, everywhere she looked all she could see were the most terrifying creatures and in the place of Chris was Emily who was smiling in a most evil way and laughing as if in victory, completely overwhelmed by the horrible sights Katrina let out a blood curdling scream and collapsed. Katrina woke up a few hours later her head pounding, once she got her bearings she noticed she was in the school medical bay the room was long and looked like an old hospital ward, looking around she saw Ms Greystone talking with the school nurse "Ugh what happened to me and what am I doing here" she asked sounding very groggy and feeling it too "You had an accident it seems you were slipped a very nasty potion that caused some terrible hallucinations" Ms Greystone replied "You were lucky Mr Summers was there at the time he saw you were in trouble and brought you here so we could administer the anti-potion" she said pointing to Chris who was sound asleep on the chair next to the bed. Katrina sat up and said very assuredly "I know who did this

to me, it was Emily she must have used a glamour spell to change her appearance"
"Yes dear we know she put some of her own magic into the potion it was almost like she wanted us to know it was her but I'm not sure why" Ms Greystone replied now very confused. Katrina looked at Ms Greystone and said very seriously "I know why she was sending a message that she can get me whenever she wants, well I know what to tell her" she got up and moved to the mirror "Bring it on you vindictive little witch if it's a fight you want then you've got it" Katrina shouted at the mirror knowing somehow that Emily was listening in.

Chapter 11

The equinox had come and gone and the students quickly got out of party mode and went into study mode, especially Katrina who really hit the books any spare time she had she was either studying for exams or figuring out new ways to get Emily, this sadly didn't leave much time for her and Chris and he was starting to feel it. Failing again to pull Katrina away from her books Chris decided to give up and go for a walk to clear his head, he decided to go to the gardens where he felt really relaxed and in his element, while out he heard something wonderful that sounded like singing and decided to go investigate. Chris followed the voice and found himself by the lake where he saw the most beautiful girl, she has long golden hair, ocean blue eyes and was wearing a ling white dress, Chris walked closer and noticed she was looking at him "Uh hi I'm Chris your song it was beautiful" he said to the girl stuttering like it was the first time he ever spoke to a girl in his life. The mystery girl gave a coy giggle and said in a voice as beautiful as her song "Oh I'm glad you liked it my name is Serena would you like to join me?" Chris obliged without any delay. The two talked for quite a while about music and other unimportant things, then quite out of character Chris said "So I was going for a walk around the grounds would you care to join me?" Serena smiled at Chris and said in her usual sweet tone "I'd love to join you but sadly I can't leave the lake" Chris looked a little confused "what do you mean why can't you leave?" Serena lifted the base of her dress and in the place of her legs was a golden tail. Chris just stared in sheer amazement and finally managed to say "Wow ok so um you're a mermaid" "Yep does this freak you out" Serena asked looking slightly sad "No way this is amazing I've always wanted to meet a mermaid I mean your such amazingly beautiful creatures" Chris said not fully realising he was flirting, Serena looked at him and blushed "Aww your sweet you know that" "I'm serious and you have an equally beautiful voice" Chris said continuing his flirtation "Ok now your just being way too charming but I really don't mind" Serena replied, to ensure she kept Chris in place Serena started humming a very hypnotic tune.

Elsewhere in the school Katrina was sitting among a large pile of books trying to balance her school work and her apparently futile search for Emily when suddenly she was hit with this strange sensation like she knew Chris was in trouble, ignoring how strange it seemed Katrina put her research aside and went straight for her grimoire and starting looking for a spell. It took a little while but she found it *The Spell to Find a Loved One*, wasting no time at all Katrina grabbed the small cauldron from her desk and proceeded to add the ingredients from the book, *a quartz crystal, Hyacinth, Jasmin, Thyme, Lotus and Picture of the one you seek*. Once all the ingredients were placed in Katrina began the chant "**Spirit aid my troubled mind the one I love please help me find. Let this mighty spell of detection allow me to give some form of protection. Spirits heed my invocation reveal to me his exact location**" as the final words were said the potion began to bubble and a flash of blinding green light filled the room, when the light faded Katrina saw her spell had worked, she could see Chris as clear as day in the mirror "Wow it worked it actually worked" she said sounding very proud that is until she saw Serena "I don't believe it that jerk he's with another girl oh he is so dead" full of rage and fury Katrina mustered up her powers and transported to where Chris was.

Katrina emerged from her teleporting spell and found herself in the right place for once, still infuriated Katrina stomped to the lake and proceeded to telekinetically throw Chris a good fifty feet across the field and strapped Serena to a tree nearby using some vines as rope, Katrina walked up to Serena and said in a very angry and forceful tone "Now listen here fish breath you go after my boyfriend again and I swear I will turn you into a spicy tuna roll are we clear" Serena didn't answer she just nodded now looking very scared. Chris ran over and yelled "Are you nuts, why did you attack her?" "Well excuse me" Katrina yelled back "I'd much rather have a living boyfriend than a dead one" Chris looked at her confused "What are you on about she's a mermaid and mermaids are friendly" "Yes you are right but she is not a mermaid" Katrina retorted "Note the tail she still has one" now Chris was really getting confused "When mermaids go on land they are granted legs but sirens their twisted cousins don't" Katrina explained. It took a few moments but Chris finally clicked on what Katrina was saying "Wait a minute you mean I've been talking with a siren the whole time"

"More like flirting if you ask me" Katrina snapped "She was seducing you with her hypnotic song" "Actually I wasn't, I tried believe me I tried, but for some reason he was immune he just kept blabbing on and on about you" Serena admitted. Hearing this Katrina stated blushing "Hey how did you know he was in trouble anyway" Serena asked now curious "Honestly I have no idea I was just in my room then I got this weird feeling in my heart and I knew" Katrina replied still confused about what she felt "Ugh well that explains it you guys have true love something even my magic can't mess with" Serena replied now sounding very upset at her failure. After everything was sorted Katrina and Chris helped Serena back into the water Katrina couldn't help but ask "Can I ask who sent you here to try and get Chris, I mean it is very rare for a siren to be out of the ocean" "Yeah no kidding you can't imagine what this lake water is doing to my skin, and honestly I have no idea just some random chick wanting to cause trouble I think her name was Emily" Serena replied. As the young couple watched Serena swim through an underwater portal Katrina looked to Chris nervously "She isn't going to stop is she we will never be safe" Chris saw her worry and said in his most reassuring tone "Don't worry about that evil witch she can throw all she has at us but we aren't going to give up", Katrina looked at him and was sadly not convinced "How can you be so sure I mean you've seen how powerful she is"

"Yeah that's true but we have something she defiantly does not have" Chris replied, Katrina looked at him and wondered what his answer would be "She doesn't have someone to love but we do and our power heck our love is much stronger than any of her spells" Katrina looked at Chris and knew he was just being sappy but it was exactly what she needed to hear. Once the two had calmed down they decided to walk back to school and try and forget their insane day.

Chapter 12

It was that time of year again, a time that every single student hated, Exam time. But they did things a little differently at Witchfield Academy; instead of long dull multiple choice questions the exams were practical, this was to show how much the students knew and to see if they could control the magic they created. Katrina had gotten through most of her exams with no problem, now there was a problem. The one exam she had been dreading, her potions exam.

The students filed into the exam hall each looking more nervous than the last; Katrina though seemed to be the most nervous one of all. As the students registered with the examiner they were each given a sealed envelope containing their assignments, once the students received their respective envelopes they made their way to their assigned desks. When the time came the examiner, a rather stern looking witch spoke "All right students on entering you were each given a sealed envelope containing your individual potion exams, when I say, you may open them and begin" the students all nodded to confirm their understanding. When the time came to begin Katrina hesitantly opened her envelope and found to her shock and horror her assignment **Enlarging Potion** *"Oh you have got to be kidding me"* Katrina thought to herself *"of all the potions I had to get this one"* she realised quickly it wouldn't do to get upset so Katrina decided to buckle down and start working. It was coming to the end of the exam and Katrina had mixed the potion rather confidently that is until the final ingredient *"Oh great which one is it again?"* now she was starting to panic trying to remember her first potion class and what the right ingredient was, then suddenly it hit her like a flash *"That's it, Knotweed, I remember now"* she thought, now very happy that she remembered and just in time too.

Time was up and the potions were starting to be tested, some of them where undeniable successes, while some where complete flops, and now it was Katrina's turn. When the examiner reached Katrina's work station she snapped up Katrina's sheet and announced the assignment "Enlarging potion simple enough, well let's see how you did" she said rather sharp and forcefully, complying with the order Katrina placed three drops on the apple on her desk, then the apple began to grow until it was the size of a basketball and then stopped. To Katrina's amazement the potion worked and this time nothing went boom "Well done Miss Woods you brewed up a very potent batch I am pleased to say you have passed" the examiner said giving a very slight smile, once the examiner moved to the next student Katrina just sat down and gave a huge sigh of relief and once it was all over Katrina left with a huge sense of accomplishment.

After the exam Katrina and Chris made arrangements to meet at their usual spot, the whole way there Katrina's head was filled with wonderfully happy thoughts. Suddenly Katrina's head started pounding, before she knew what was happening she saw the most horrific sights. She saw herself, Chris and all the teachers and students lying on the ground struggling to keep alive, and the school burning in the background. Worst of all she saw Emily standing over the whole scene laughing victoriously. As the laughter became deafening Katrina snapped out of her vision and luckily fell into Chris' arms "Whoa you ok" Chris asked as Katrina was starting to come around "No I'm not I think I just had a vision" she replied starting to panic, "Hey try and relax, witches get visions all the time you don't need to panic" "We all need to panic" Katrina said "I saw everyone dying and the school was in ruins" "Oh god that is awful" Chris replied now feeling a little scared himself. " It gets worse I saw Emily, and she was standing over everything laughing at it all" Chris was now silent and he was really getting nervous but was not showing it "We are in serious trouble aren't we" Katrina said tears starting to fill her eyes, Chris saw Katrina's sadness and gave her a tight hug trying to soothe her.

Sadly their tender moment was cut short by a large storm that appeared out of nowhere, "Oh man this storm is insane I can hardly see anything" Chris yelled over the storms booming noise "This is Emily's doing I know it is she's trying to freak us out" Katrina yelled also straining to see Chris through the rain. She was right of course as Emily couldn't resist manifesting herself in one of the cloud formations "Oh how sad, the little couple can't find each other, well let me help" and with that the storm stopped as if it was never there.

"That's weird why, would she want to help us" Chris asked now very confused. But before an answer could be given a small portal opened up right under Chris' feet and he was quickly dragged into its pull. Shocked and horrified by what she had just seen Katrina started screaming at the now empty sky "Bring him back, you bring him back right now you evil witch" "Oh don't worry my dear" Emily's voice echoed "You will be with him soon enough" and with that Katrina was pulled into the oblivion of a portal just like Chris.

Chapter 13

The young couple awoke and found themselves in the courtyard of a ruined castle "Ah good your awake I was starting to get bored" echoed a voice coming from nowhere, even in her confused state Katrina recognised the voice instantly "Emily" she called to the air "I should have figured you would pull some stunt like this I'm almost impressed" "Are you insane first rule in these things is don't tick off the crazy voice" urged Chris finally catching on to the situation. Katrina just smiled "Oh please she doesn't scare me she is just some washed up old crone with a serious attitude problem" she said in her most venomous tone trying to flush Emily out. To no one's surprise the ploy worked, Emily appeared to them in a swirl of purple smoke and emerged looking both furious and determined. Her outfit most certainly matched her attitude, she wore a full length black dress with silver sewn through and her hair in a long ponytail "Now listen here you little brat I have more power in one little finger than you have in your entire body" replied Emily now starting to lose her temper.

After a several minutes of verbal sparring Katrina finally asked the question that had been bugging her for months "Why are you doing all of this what did I do to you" "It isn't you I'm after you silly twit it's your necklace I want after all it should be mine" replied Emily sounding extremely venomous, "I don't get it the necklace always goes to the eldest child how can you be entitled?" Katrina asked very confused by Emily's claim. Emily took a moment after hearing the question and replied in her angriest voice ever "I am Antonia's older sister so that necklace should be mine" Chris and Katrina both looked in total shock at the revelation "No you must be lying how is this possible it must be a sick joke" replied Katrina trying very hard to process this new and shocking information, Emily could not wait and told her tragic tale.

Our mother was of common birth but she wanted more much more, she had her sights set on being a noble woman but of course that meant marrying a noble man, and she thought she found her perfect match in a man named Victor. Sadly she was wrong, Victor was not a noble man but a servant who stole his masters' clothes and impersonated him. Mother found out too late as she was already expecting me, after I was born my mother abandoned me in the woods, I was lucky a forest witch found me and took me in. she taught me most of the basics the rest I learned over the years, I never forgot my mother in fact I found her and confronted her, she denied it all of course until I showed her a scrap from my blanket then she knew. She was pathetic trying to explain herself, but I listened to her pathetic tale then I turned her into a statue and quickly smashed her into a thousand pieces. Oh believe me I was pleased but the pleasure was short lived once I found out about my sister and the necklace that should have been mine, and well history told the rest of our family squabble.

Katrina though still in shock from the whole thing but managed to snap out enough to say "History said you perished in the battle how are you still alive" "It was a miracle I survived I was very close to death but managed to escape barely" Emily replied rather forcefully "But that was centuries ago how can you still be alive?" Chris asked now rather curious himself "I have been stealing the life force of other witches to keep myself young and powerful, quite the beauty regime huh" Emily retorted this time sounding very proud of her wicked actions, "But enough chit chat hand over the necklace" "Not a chance" Katrina yelled clutching the necklace "Fine have it your own way I guess I will just have to take it" Emily replied rather forcefully, throwing a fireball at Chris and Katrina. Thankfully the couple dodged the attack and moved to a safer ground "Is that the best you've got you withered old crone" shouted Katrina as she hurled a light dart in Emily's direction "Are you out of your mind" Chris whispered "she is several centuries old witch who can wipe us out in a flash" he had suddenly lost his usual cool attitude and was looking very scared. Emily heard this and took full advantage of the fear "You should listen to him sweetie if you think I'm bad just wait my friends are much worse" before the young couple could even take stock of what was said Emily began chanting a very dark spell **"Creatures of darkness minions of hell I call you now with this spell. Rise up from your ancient tomb and bring about these fools doom"** as the final words were spoken large clouds of black smoke filled the fields and a vast army of dark and hideous creatures emerged, and they had their sights set on Katrina and Chris.

The fight had begun, Chris and Katrina used every spell they knew to fight off Emily's shadow creatures, and as luck would have it they were winning. Seeing her enemies distracted Emily cast one of the darkest spells in history *the shadow ball of death*, one hit and it's all over. Focusing her power Emily fired the attack directly at Katrina, seeing the attack Chris cast a deflector spell and threw the attack off course. Seeing her attack fail Emily vanished in her usual purple smoke this time more violently. Once he was sure it was safe Chris ran over to Katrina and gave her a very deep kiss "You know you really know how to scare a guy" he said laughing slightly "Sorry I seem to attract trouble, well it looks like it's over" Katrina said relieved, but before another word could be spoken a second shadow ball flew through the air and caught Chris right between the shoulders "Ha got him, oh I can't believe you actually thought I was gone" Emily cheered in a cruel and shrill voice.

As Katrina looked at the cold lifeless body of the man she loved she let out a shrill scream that caused the entire castle to shake, then the most astounding thing happened. Katrina's entire body was consumed in a blinding white light, once the light faded Katrina was completely transformed. Her hair was as white as snow and her eyes had become the most intense fire red you could ever see, Emily knew what it meant her enemy had been raised to the form of Grand White Witch, it also meant she was in big trouble. After taking a moment to adjust to her new powers, Katrina then stood before Emily's army, raised her hand and said in a terrifying echoed voice "**Minions of darkness be gone**" with that a fierce beam of power swept the battlefields obliterating all of the shadow creatures.

After seeing that amazing feat of power Emily realised instantly that she would be next, and the only thing left for her to do was grovel to save her skin "Well I must say that was impressive, and your new look love it. Well since you don't need me I'll be off" she said as she quickly turned heel to run. Unfortunately for her Katrina used a binding spell which locked Emily where she stood "Nice try you old crone but I'm not done with you" she pointed to Chris's body "Bring him back now or I swear you will suffer" Katrina said in her harshest voice "Oh I wish I could sweetie but resurrection isn't one of my strong suits sadly your boy toy is gone" Emily replied sounding surprisingly sincere "Regardless you will need to pay for your crimes" stated Katrina still sounding forceful "Of course whatever you deem necessary" Emily replied. Katrina took a moment to come to grips with the horrible situation, that one moment was all Emily needed to break Katrina's binding spell "Ha I can't believe you actually fell for that old routine, boy you really are stupid" sneered Emily "Do you really think I give a troll's backside that your boyfriend is dead, he is just collateral damage, all I care about is beating you and getting what is mine". As she finished Emily conjured a large fireball and sent it hurling in Katrina's direction. Seeing this Katrina raised her hands and sent the attack rebounding back to its caster, before she could even react Emily became consumed by the force of the spell and burst into flames, her agonising screams echoed until she was no more than a pile of ashes.

After watching Emily's demise Katrina reverted to her natural form and broke down crying over Chris's body "I am so sorry Chris this is all my fault, oh I wish I knew a way to bring you back" she said through tear filled eyes her voice breaking with each tragic word "Fear not child, all is not lost there is a way" announced an invisible voice "Who said that" Katrina announced sounding rather nervous "I did" replied the voice now appearing in front of Katrina. It took Katrina a moment to fully realise what was happening "You … Your Antonia aren't you" she said still shaking at the apparition floating in front of her "Yes I am dear please do not worry I am here to offer my help" the spirit spoke her voice soft with a slight echo to it "Oh really you're here to help where have you been up until now huh I could have used your help" Katrina yelled now enraged "My dear please understand I have tried to communicate with you all year but my sisters dark magic was blocking my attempts. The few times I did get through the messages became distorted" Antonia explained, hearing this Katrina realised it seemed to make sense all of the visions and the crystal ball incident all started to come together. It took some time but Katrina managed to come to terms with everything, and once her composure she returned she looked at Antonia and asked "So how do we do this, I always read to bring someone else back someone else needs to die" "That is normally the case but a few clever witches created resurrection spells that do not require a life to be given, instead you must sacrifice something of great personal value and power" Antonia explained seeming very serious. Katrina just looked at her and realised what she meant "My necklace?" Antonia nodded "So to get Chris back I need to give up the power in my necklace" Antonia nodded again "Yes that is the price of the spell are you willing to make the sacrifice" "Absolutely I don't care about the power I want Chris back no matter what" Katrina announced now sounding very determined.

It took a few minutes but Katrina managed to memorize the spell Antonia spoke of, Katrina knelt next to Chris and raised her amulet into the air and began chanting "**Ancient spirits from high above restore to life the one I love. Bring light to this dark over in sacrifice take this items power**", as the spell was completed the colour and power drained from the amulet and poured into Chris. It took a moment but once all the power was gone Chris awoke with a loud gasp, seeing her success Katrina grabbed Chris and gave him a large hug and showered him with kisses "Oh I can't believe it your back your actually back" she said overjoyed "Back what are you talking about did I go somewhere?" Chris asked now extremely confused "I'll tell you later" Katrina replied laughing slightly "Let's just get out of here and I'll explain everything" with that Katrina helped Chris up and tried to find a way back to the school.

Epilogue

Katina and Chris made it back to the school with no problem, it was odd but the two of them couldn't be happier to be back at school of all places. Katrina used their long walk through the corridors to fill him in on the events he missed, his reaction was what you would expect sheer confusion "So your trying to tell me that I was dead" he said trying to wrap his head around the situation and failing miserably "Yes you were and I used magic to bring you back" Katrina said with a slight tone of pride in her voice. Chris was awe struck by the whole thing then realised something "Wait how can I be back to bring someone back from the dead someone else has to die, please tell me you didn't do anything crazy" he asked now very nervous "Don't worry no one was used to bring you back, but there was a high price" Katrina said rather solemnly. Chris was about to quiz Katrina further on what she said, but before he could he saw his answer. Katrina's necklace still hanging from her neck was different, instead of its usual fiery red it was now plain and void of any colour or power. On seeing this Chris just looked at her and said trying hard to be composed "You mean you gave up the power in your necklace to bring me back" Katrina just nodded, seeing the confirmation Chris started tearing up a little "You know I can't believe you, you actually gave all that power up for me" "Well believe it buster and I would do it again without thinking" Katrina replied smiling and hugging him close. After everything was explained Katrina and decided they had better to Ms Greystone and fill her in, a situation neither one of them was looking forward to.

When the two reached Ms Greystone's office door they decide to be polite and knock this time, but before they could they were swept into the office and stopped right in front of the headmistresses desk and she did not look pleased "Well you two have a lot of explaining to do, I trust you have a good reason for being off campus during school hours and not even bothering to leave a note" yes Ms Greystone was indeed furious "Yes we do have a good reason for this but it is hard to explain" Katrina answered sounding confident

"Please do try Ms Woods and it better be good" the headmistress replied still infuriated. Chris and Katrina sat and both began explain every single detail of their adventure making sure not to miss anything, when done Ms Greystone looked at them with a look of total shock "Good heavens this is astounding, and considering the events of today you two are excused from the rest of your exams now go and rest. But Mr Summers visit the school nurse first just so she can check you over" Ms Greystone ordered her voice shaking a little.

The two left Ms Greystone and followed her instructions, Chris went to the school nurse for a full check-up and thankfully he was given a clean bill of health apart from a large bruise between his shoulders. Katrina on the other hand went straight to her room and immediately called her parents to explain things mainly the part about who Emily really was and what she had done to her necklace, thankfully her mother was not upset about the necklace quite the opposite in fact she was proud of her daughter for doing something so selfless, the only thing she couldn't get her head around was the face Katrina's roommate was their insane ancestor. The news of Chris and Katrina's exploits quickly spread through the entire school and the two became the talk of the school, of course they didn't care about all that they were just glad it was all over, and as far as they knew it was.